For EEE

THIS IS A BORZOI BOOK PUBLISHED BY ALFRED A. KNOPF

Copyright © 2017 by Maxwell Eaton III

All rights reserved. Published in the United States by Alfred A. Knopf, an imprint of Random House Children's Books, a division of Penguin Random House LLC, New York.
Knopf, Borzoi Books, and the colophon are registered trademarks of Penguin Random House LLC.
Visit us on the Web! randomhousekids.com   Educators and librarians, for a variety of teaching tools, visit us at RHTeachersLibrarians.com

Library of Congress Cataloging-in-Publication Data
Names: Eaton, Maxwell, author. Title: I'm awake! / Maxwell Eaton III. Other titles: I am awake
Description: First edition. | New York : Alfred A. Knopf, [2017] |
Identifiers: LCCN 2016009555 | ISBN 978-0-375-84575-8 (trade) | ISBN 978-0-375-94575-5 (lib. bdg.) | ISBN 978-0-553-53387-3 (ebook)
Subjects: | CYAC: Morning—Fiction. | Father and child—Fiction. Summary: "An energetic young critter tries to coax his dad out of bed in the morning." —Provided by publisher
The illustrations in this book were created using pen and ink with digital coloring. Classification: LCC PZ7.E3892 Im 2017 | DDC [E]—dc23

MANUFACTURED IN CHINA   May 2017   10 9 8 7 6 5 4 3 2 1   First Edition
Random House Children's Books supports the First Amendment and celebrates the right to read.

W9-CBR-502